Born in Salisbury, Wiltshire in 1961, the son of a steam train driver, he left school at 16 and started work in the Post Office as a telegram boy. At 18 he became a postman. He left after 7 years, and followed his father on the railway. He is now retired with a railway pension and lives in Hampshire.

THE QUEST

R.J. Haywood

Austin Macauley Publishers™
London • Cambridge • New York • Sharjah

A CIP catalogue record for this title is available from the British Library.

ISBN 9781035832415 (Paperback)
ISBN 9781035832422 (Hardback)
ISBN 9781035832439 (ePub e-book)

www.austinmacauley.com

First Published 2024
Austin Macauley Publishers Ltd®
1 Canada Square
Canary Wharf
London
E14 5AA

To Isla,
Whose kind words encouraged me to go ahead and see if I could get my story published.

To all the hardworking bees which inspired me to write this book.

Chapter 1
The Summoning

The Queen Bee is sat on her throne, she has just summoned her four bravest bees into court. She has some grave news to share with them and a mission for them to undertake. She then instructs one of her staff to show them in.

Meanwhile, the four bees are outside the hives court, waiting to be introduced to the Queen. None of them have seen the Queen for a very long time; she has become a bit of a recluse.

As they stand there, all four of them wonder why they have been summoned. They gaze at each other, feeling like four mischievous school bees. Eventually, they are led into court, and they find the Queen bee seated in front of them.

She looks awful, but you could not tell her that, as you would be expelled from the hive, and then, what would you do? If you tried to join another hive, they would want references and throw you out for telling the Queen that she looked awful. Well, your days would be numbered. So, there they are, standing in front of the Queen. At first she says nothing, she just looks at them one by one. First at Hornbee, he is the biggest of the four bees, he is two whole millimetres bigger than Frizzbee and Freebee and three millimetres bigger than Tobee. He is what we would call a big bumblebee.

Hornbee does not say a lot, but when he does, it is straight to the point. He is a no-nonsense type of bee.

Then the Queen looks at Frizzbee and Freebee, who are twins. They are very brave, but there is a fine line between being brave and being foolhardy.

There is a saying that fools rush in where angels fear to tread; well, that sums up Frizzbee and Freebee: brave to the point of being reckless.

They are often by each other's side, and when they speak, it is often in unison, which can seem rather strange.

Then finally, she looks at Tobee; he is the youngest and the smallest of the four; he is very active and quick-thinking; he is by no means anybody's fool; and is well respected by his elders.

Then the Queen speaks, as you can see, one is not well. My illness has been going on for some time, which is why I have become a recluse. My doctors have informed me that this is because the giant two-legged creatures (the humans) have sprayed poison (insecticide) on the flowers and con-taminated the pollen.

Unless pure pollen that has not been tainted by the two-legged creatures can be found, i will die"

The four bees can hardly believe what they are hearing, if the Queen dies the whole hive will suffer, they are supported by her.

Frizzbee and Freebee both turn pale at this news, and then the Queen announces that she will send all four bees out in separate directions, one North, one East, one West and one South. Frizzbee and Freebee don't like the idea of being separated, but they know they must do this. So, they decide to draw straws to see who goes in which direction. The longest straw goes North, the second longest East, the third longest West, and the shortest goes South. The Queen holds out the four straws in her hands. Hornbee goes first and pulls out the second longest straw (he will be going East). Then it's Frizzbee's turn; he pulls out the third longest straw (he will be going West). Then Freebee has a go and pulls out the longest straw (he will be going North). That leaves Tobee with the shortest straw, which is South. Then the Queen says, "Very well, you have your orders. Good luck and good speed," and beckons them to leave. Once outside the hive, all four bees look back at their home and the surrounding lands,

knowing they may never see them again. Then all four, with a tear in their eye, say goodbye to each other and proceed on their quest.

Chapter 2
The Queen

It was a sunny day when the Queen sent the four bees out on their quest. She sat on her throne and watched the door shut behind them. She knew that their mission could be perilous, but what choice did she have? And now that she was alone, she started to weep, after all they were her children. The Queen became a recluse as soon as she realised that she was becoming gravely ill, she did not want the hive to get into a panic if they were to see her so ill, so the only bees that were allowed to see her were her doctors, of course, and her immediate servants, who were sworn to secrecy.

And now the deed was done—she had sent Hornbee, Frizzbee, Freebee, and Tobee out to the four corners of the world. She had delayed her actions for some time, but the doctors had told her she had no choice, for there was nothing they could do for her; only pure pollen could save her and the hive.

She is a well-loved Queen who was always known for having a good heart. She always had time to speak to her subjects and was never full of self-importance, but she knew her duty to the hive. In recent times, some of the younger bees' memories of the Queen were very faded due to her seclusion. Therefore, it was left to the older bees to tell them what a lovely Queen she is, no one had a bad word to say about her.

After a while when all her tears had dried up, she rose from her throne and walked very slowly to her bedchamber. She was becoming very weak due to the poison running through her body, and she was in great pain. However, she did her

best to hide it from the four bees.

When she got to her bedchamber, she laid down and tried to get a little sleep, to dream of better times when she was young, and healthy, and full of joy.

She woke up covered in sweat and looked out of the hive. She saw that the sun was rising, and she realised she had slept for about twelve hours.

Her bedchamber was quite sparse, as bees are not materialistic. Feeling quite thirsty, she took a sip of some water That had been left in a bowl for her. After quenching her thirst, she thought of her children, who had never been far from her mind.

Chapter 3
Hornbee Goes East

When Hornbee left the hive, the sun was shining, but he knew it was not likely to stay that way; at some point, it was bound to rain or even snow. Hornbee does not like the snow; in fact, no bees do; they much prefer the warmer climate.

After a day of flying east, Hornbee has not come across any other bees. He finds this quite disturbing and starts to wonder if his hive is the only one left. Then he comes across a hive with a sentry at the front; he flies down and introduces himself. Bees are very social; they always have time to speak to other bees, even if they are from a different hive. The sentry tells him his name is Crombee. Hornbee tells him of his quest.

Crombee is also a big bumblebee who is about the same size as Hornbee.

He tells him that some of the hives Queens have died, and that the other hives have taken in their bees, but some of them mourned their Queens so much that they died of a broken heart.

Hornbee suggests that their hive should send bees out in search of pure pollen. Crombee tells him that he will inform his superiors as soon as his sentry duty is over, as wasps have realised the weakened state of the bees and have attacked some of the hives.

Bees and wasps don't get along; where bees are quite gentle in nature, wasps are always out to cause trouble and to be a bother.

Hornbee realises he must crack on; there is nothing for him here, so Hornbee and Crombee bid farewell to each other and wish each other good luck.

After a while, Hornbee notices that the wind is picking up

to such a degree that he is starting to struggle with his flying; it is coming straight at him, then it starts to get stronger and stronger to the point where he is hardly making any progress at all.

Then the wind changes direction and starts to blow him from left to right. He sees a bale of hay down below and decides to take cover and sleep there for the night.

He burrows himself deep within the bale of hay, where it is nice and warm. Once inside, he decides to have a bit to eat, so he prepares some flower petals mixed with herbs. After he had finished that, he then has a little bit of sugar washed down with some water, and then he lays down to get some sleep. He is totally exhausted. In the morning, Hornbee is feeling quite refreshed. He looks out onto the world and sees that it has been raining during the night, but the sun was now shining, and it looked like it was going to be a beautiful day.

So, he sets off, and after a while, he starts to feel a slight breeze, but nothing serious. Then he notices he is by the coast.

There is a solitary flower there, so he tries the pollen and sees that it is infected. You see, when a bee has infected pollen on the back of his legs (that's where he stores it), when he touches another flower that has not been infected, he unknowingly infects the flower. Hornbee looks out over the sea. He knows he has too somehow cross it, but how?

Chapter 4
Frizzbee Goes West

Frizzbee felt quite empty inside at the thought of being separated from his brother. After travelling a couple of miles, he sat down on a rock (he was feeling quite sad), he sat there for a hour just looking at the sky and the land, then he pulled himself together and moved on.It was sunny when he left the hive, but the further west he went the cloudier it became, although it was not cold. In fact, the temperature was very mild, and the landscape became quite open, with fields that spread out for miles, with rocky coastlines that have deer, rabbits, pheasants, and all sorts of wildlife.

Frizzbee thought" Maybe I have found the promised land," so he flies down where he spots a honeysuckle bush. He just wants to dive down and bathe in its pollen, but as soon as he touches the honeysuckle, he can tell that the pollen is infected.

Frizzbee is overcome with despair, "Why on earth do the two-legged creatures do this, what good can come from it?"

The clouds start to disperse, and the sun breaks through. Frizzbee feel the sun on his back, and the warmth gives him the motivation to move on.

Although male bees are thought to be very brave, they very rarely leave the surrounding area of the hive. However extreme situations call for extreme measures.

Frizzbee comes across an apple orchard; he could do with something to eat, so he finds a juicy apple and takes in its sweet and juicy flesh. while there, he spots a female bee; she seems so busy that she does not seem to notice him. Frizzbee feels a sort of curiosity towards her; no, it's more than that —it's an attraction.

Then he spots a hornet on the ground quite near to where

the female bee is flying; he is filled with horror. He must act quickly. He flies down to her and puts a finger in front of his lips to indicate silence. Then he points down to where the hornet is, and they both head for cover in the nearest bush.

Frizzbee then gets quite stern with her, don't you keep your eyes open when you are flying about. "Hornets will kill you as soon as they see you," she replies, saying, "Well, what's it to do with you?" in a terse manner.

Frizzbee tells her that he was worried for her. She sees that he is now feeling awkward at saying this. She then, in a much softer voice, tells him that he is right and that she is sorry. She then gives him a kiss on the cheek.

If bee's could blush then Frizzbee would of done,

she giggles at his embarrassment and tells him her name is Debbee. Frizzbee smiles and introduces himself. She wants to know all about him, so he tells her of the quest and how the four of them set out, and that he has a twin brother called Freebee who has gone north, she informs him that some time ago their hive was stricken with the sickness, and they thought that their Queen would die, but she recovered along with the rest of the bees.

They then sat and talked for the rest of the day; they then held hands and kissed; and they stayed there that night in each other's arms, staring at the stars.

In the morning, Frizzbee tells her he must move on with his search; after all, he is under orders from his Queen. He asks her if she would come here every day at midday and wait for his return; she promises that she will. They then embrace, and then Frizzbee flies off feeling as light as a feather.

Chapter 5
Freebee Goes North

Freebee, upon leaving the hive, is also unhappy about leaving his brother. However, he thinks to himself, "The sooner I set off, the sooner I can get back. I must stay positive," so he sets off with the wind at his back. After travelling for some miles, his spirits become quite cheerful, and he starts to hum a tune, to us this sounds like a buzzing sound.

The sun is high, and the fields are green with cows and sheep grazing. it all looks very beautiful. He sees a stream down below and decides to take a drink and to rest up for a few minutes. His thoughts turn to his brother, and he is wondering how he is coping. But he says to himself, "I must not dwell on things." so he decides to push on north. He wipes his lips and set off once more. The further he goes, the colder it seems to get. He puts this down to the fact that it is approaching the end of the day. He looks around for somewhere warm to rest up for the night and sees an old barn. He flies down to investigate. upon entering the barn, he looks around the barn and it is totally empty and cold. The only thing in there is spiders and their cobwebs, that seem to be covering most of the interior of the building. Freebee thinks to himself, "I don't want to end up caught in one of their webs. This will not do whatsoever," So he turns around and heads back out.

So, he continues further north. He is starting to get a bit concerned as the sun is starting to go down and it is getting colder by the minute. Suddenly, he spots a cottage. He looks all around it for an opening and finds a little hole in the tiled roof. He flies down and puts his head inside. It's is so lovely

and warm in there, with roof insulation that he can cover himself up in to keep warm while he sleeps.

The next morning, after a lovely snooze. The first thought on his mind is breakfast, so he has a good stretch and looks out onto the surrounding garden of the cottage. He spots a plum tree, plums and strawberries happens to be Freebee's favourite fruit. He flies down and finds a plum that is not too hard. He eagerly tastes its delicious flesh, but he eats it so quickly that he ends up making a mess. His face and body are covered in plum juice, and he feels sticky. Spotting a puddle, he washes himself in it and then tries the pollen from the garden flowers. Unfortunately, he realizes that it's infected, which brings him back down to earth in terms of his mission. So, he sets off once more on his quest.

Now, with every mile he travels, the landscape seems to change from grasslands and woods to tarmac roads and concrete structures. Freebee does not like this environment; he thinks it looks ugly. However, he presses on, and now there are cars and busses, along with big tall buildings and big chimneys billowing out smoke everywhere. There is hardly any grass or trees to be seen anywhere. Freebee thinks to himself, "How can these two-legged creatures live like this? Where is there love for Mother Nature?"

While travelling through this land of concrete and smoke, Freebee develops a slight cough and thinks to himself, "The sooner I get through this land the better," so he goes on and on through the smoke and grime of the city, and his cough is getting worse. However, up ahead, he can see a clearing. He flies as fast as he can to reach it. Finally, there are trees, grass, plants and even a pond. Freebee flies down by the side of the pond, where some ducks are splashing about. He is feeling very weak now and his cough is almost continuous.

Then another bee spots him on the ground and hears his coughing. She flies down to him and introduces herself as Rubee, she says to him, "You had better come with me." She takes him to her hive where she gives him some water to drink and wipes his brow. Freebee now has a temperature and he's sweating. She tells him that her hive never travels through the city anymore and that they would sooner fly around it. Then Freebee tells Rubee of the quest that he, his brother, and two other bees have been sent on. All the time Freebee is telling Rubee about this, she is wiping his brow or holding his hand. She has seen bees in this condition before when they have gone through the city. She knows that Freebee is not well.

Chapter 6
Tobee Goes South

Tobee is the youngest and most likely the fittest of the four bees. He is glad that he is going south, as the south seems to be warmer. He has never been on any adventure like this before, and though he is somewhat nervous, he is also very excited as well.

Tobee became known for his bravery when, late one summer, a wasp attacked him for no reason whatsoever. It came straight at him, and Tobee waited to the last minute as he charged at him and then dodged to one side. The wasp then crashed into a brick wall behind him, and by the time the wasp had come to his senses, Tobee had turned around and stung him.

For some reason, wasps in late summer get dopey and want to attack everyone.

The other time was when a two-legged creature came towards the hive in full white protective clothing, holding a smoke gun (bees do not like smoke: it makes them drowsy). Tobee flew down to his shoe and slowly managed to get under his trouser leg and stung him. While the two-legged creature was jumping up and down in pain, Tobee scrambled back down his leg and flew back to the hive. All the bees in the hive saw what he did, and they all considered him very brave. Tobee knows of a river that heads in a southerly direction, so he decides to follow it down; that way, he knows he has a constant supply of water. Also, before leaving, he puts some beeswax over his body to keep him fully waterproof in case it rains. Now that he had thought out his route and had prepared himself, it was time to see what this adventure had install for him.

Whilst travelling along the river, he saw a few dragonflies of different colours darting her and there. He thought to himself, "What lovely colours they have! if only they would keep still for a minute so that he could fully see them." Then he saw a fish jump out of the water and catch a fly in its mouth. Tobee thought to himself, "I better not fly directly over the water as I don't want the same fate as that fly."

He saw some pretty water lilies poking their heads out of the water. Then, to the right of him, he saw a bungalow with a red rose bush in its garden, along with some lavender growing in pots. The smells were gorgeous, so he went over to try the pollen. However, it was infected. Tobee decides he is unlikely to find pure, uninflected pollen in a two-legged creature's garden. He would be better off looking for wild flowers. But first, he must wash the infected pollen off his legs, otherwise, he will only end up infecting other flowers. So, he sees a puddle by the side of the river and flies down to wash his legs. This was harder than he thought as the pollen had stuck to the beeswax, he had smothered himself with, but eventually, he got it off.

Tobee then rested up for a while and thought about the meeting with the Queen. Being a young bee, this was the first time that he had ever seen her, due to the fact that she had been a recluse with her illness for so long. Along with the excitement of the adventure, he also felt proud that he had been chosen for this quest at such a young age. He just hoped that he would not let her down. "Well time waits for no bee" he thought to himself and got to his feet then spread his wings to fly on along the river."

The further he went the faster the pace of the river seemed to flow; this did not seem to worry a heron that he saw standing in the middle of the river, as still as a statue, looking out for fish to grab. Tobee carried on down the route of the river; it was quite cool, especially as the river had picked up such a

pace. Right in front of him, he saw a waterfall. He flew over the top and saw the water crashing down below, where the river continued to flow south. but at a slower rate. Tobee found the site of the waterfall very exhilarating, such a powerful force of nature. "What an adventure this is turning out to be."

Carrying on along the river that was now moving along at a trickle, he saw a Kingfisher perched on a branch, looking for fish, Tobee kept out of the way of him as he did not know if they would eat bees.

He had tried the pollen of a few flowers along the way, but all were infected. The day was now coming to an end, and so he had to find somewhere safe to sleep for the night. He noticed a nook in a tree that was just above him. He flew up and looked in; it was not used, so he crept in and made himself comfortable for the night. It took Tobee a little while to get off to sleep due to thinking about the things he had seen, like the heron, Kingfisher, and most of all the waterfall.

The next morning, Tobee went foraging for food. He found some mint and wild sweet pea growing by the side of the river. This with some freshwater, gave him a boost in energy, so now he flew off along the river to see what the new day had to offer.

Chapter 7
Crombee Earns His Stripes

When Crombee had finished his sentry duty, he went to his commander and told him of his meeting with Hornbee and the quest he is on. He then requested that their hive should send some of their bees on the quest for pure nectar. The commander said he would arrange a meeting with the Queen, and he will be summoned in due course.

Crombee goes back to his quarters and feels quite restless, thinking about the meeting with the Queen. Then, his commander appears at the entrance of his quarters and says "Come with me," He is marched into court to see the Queen, and there she is sat in front of him. She smiles gently at him then says "You are a good bee, Crombee, always thinking of what's good for the hive. However, I cannot let you or any of the other bees leave the hive at the moment due to the constant threat of attack from the wasps. We need every bee to be ready to defend the hive." Crombee turned to his commander for permission to speak. the commander nods his head, and Crombee replies by saying, "Yes your majesty, I fully understand." He then bows, and his commander leads him out. Crombee goes back to his quarters. He is disappointed, but he decides to put it to one side for now as he needs to get something to eat and get an early night's sleep, as he has sentry duties in the morning.

That night, Crombee is lying in his bed. He had only put his head down for about half an hour when suddenly there is an almighty noise. There is shouting and screaming. Crombee jumps out of bed and looks out of his quarters. He sees one of his colleagues running towards him (his name is Robbee). His eyes are as wide as an owl's. "The wasps are attacking!" he yells. Crombee dashes out and sees his commander, who

is getting everyone in line. He looked out to the wasps, and then he gives the order to attack. Crombee is one of the first bees to react. With his sting fully sharpened, he flies out of the hive straight towards the oncoming wasps.

The wasps are led by an unsavoury character called Spike: he does not believe in showing any mercy to his enemies. He has two generals who he rules with an iron rod; they are called Sly and Slash. He orders Sly to take his command to the left-hand flank, and Slash to take his command to the right-hand flank, whilst Spike decides to go straight down the middle with the rest of the troops.

As Crombee arrives in the battle zone, he sees a wasp coming straight at him. He parries his first thrust, then dodges his second. As he comes at him a third time Crombee waits until the last second and moves to one side, just as the wasp passes by him, he twists his body around and stings him in the back.

The wasp falls to the ground like a brick. With the next wasp, he parries his first thrust and then the second with ease. This wasp is not as fast as Crombee, so when he comes at him a third time, he quickly stings him in the ribs before the wasp could defend himself. Then, out of the blue, a wasp comes flying down out of the sky and just misses his head. This is Slash, Crombee could tell straight away that this wasp was more experienced in battle.

All around him, Crombee could see bees and wasps in airborne battle. But Crombee had to give full attention to Slash, who flew back around and sneered at Crombee. Crombee then prepared himself for another attack. Slash sways from side to side, brandishing his stinger (he is trying to intimidate Crombee), Crombee pretends to flee, and slash chases after him. Crombee then does a reverse loop (this is an extremely difficult flying manoeuvre where he has to fly back over himself) and he ends up right behind Slash, He then stings him in the

back of the neck.

Sly sees this and notices that the right-hand flank is totally beaten; his own left-hand flank has suffered many losses, so he looks over to Spike. Spike also sees what's happening and that the bees to the right are now closing in on the centre. Spike orders a retreat. A roar comes out from the bees as they realised that they have beaten back the wasps. They then help there wounded back to the hive. After this, they have the sad task of carrying the bodies of their fallen back to the hive.

Once back in the hive, Crombee takes a drink of water and starts to reflect on what he had just gone through. When the commander appears at his quarters, once more he has been summoned to see the Queen, Crombee quickly brushes himself down and follows his commander.

The Queen has a big smile on her face and praises the bravery of the bees and says, "You have all earned your stripes tonight." She then tells Crombee that she will allow him to join Hornbee on his quest, but she does not feel ready to release any of the other bees. Although she does not expect the wasps to make another attack so soon after the beating they have just received, one should never take anything for granted. She then wishes him well on his journey, Crombee then bows and is led out of court, he then prepares to leave in the morning to find Hornbee.

Chapter 8
Debbee's Dream

It had been two weeks since Frizzbee had said goodbye to Debbie. He wishes he could be by her side; he is also missing Freebee.

Over the past few days, Frizzbee has been feeling quite depressed. All the pollen seems to be infected; he is wondering if he will ever be able to return home.

He sits down on the grass and looks around for something to eat. He notices a seagull standing on a rock, it must have been the size of a cat. He has never seen such a big seagull before. It lets out a squawk, that is ear piercing and then it flies off.

Frizzbee finds some dandelions to eat and then decided to spend an hour just sitting there. His thoughts turned to Debbie; he wishes he knew more about her, things like her favourite colour, place, and flowers. He then thinks of her lovely smile and her beautiful eyes.

A fox runs by with a devious look on his face. Frizzbee thinks that he is up to no good, probably looking to steal some eggs.

He looks up at the sky; the sun is out but the clouds are starting to close in. Frizzbee knows he must carry on with his travels. He gets to his feet and off he went.

After a couple of miles, he sees an old tin mine that has been abandoned for many years. To Frizzbee, this is just another scar on the face of the earth caused by the two-legged creatures. It is starting to rain, and it will start to get dark in a few hours. So, Frizzbee looks for shelter to hold up for the night. He flies on and finds a cluster of boulders. He crawls in under them and climes halfway up, where it is dry and warm.

For a week, Debbie has returned to the apple orchard every day, hoping to see Frizzbee.

On the morning he left to continue with his quest, she went back to her hive and was absolutely buzzing with joy from her lovely time with Frizzbee. She did not tell anyone in her hive about her relationship with Frizzbee, in case she was looked upon as a silly little bee. She had only just met him; how could her feelings for him be so strong?

She thought they would laugh at her and say he would not return, and that he was just playing with her emotions. She waited at the apple orchard for some time, and there was no sign of Frizzbee. So, she went back to her hive feeling a bit lonely as she was longing to see him.

That night, she went to bed and started to dream about Frizzbee saving her life by fighting the hornet and beating him off, even though the hornet was more than twice his size. She then dreamt of kissing him on the lips, then her dream turned to wishing that he was immune to the effects of the infected pollen, just like her hive was. She woke up with a jolt, and that's it.

Could her hive give some of their blood to Frizzbee's hive through an injection? Would this help to make them immune as well?

The next morning, she flies over to see the hives doctor. She tells him all about Frizzbee, his quest, and her idea of a blood transfusion. The doctor tells her to slow down as she is going into unknown territory. He explained that they would have to take some of Frizzbee's blood, along with some of theirs, and put it together in a test tube to see if it will work. They also needed to check if our immune system will remain strong when mixed with his blood. The doctor said he would present this idea to the hive council, who would then decide if it should be brought to the Queen for her consideration. He assured her that he would recommend it for trials. She

thanks the doctor then flies back to her quarters. She is not going to wait for the permission, so she leaves a note on her bed and flies off to find Frizzbee.

Chapter 9
The Forest

As Tobee flies alongside the river, he sees that it is winding towards a forest. This looks very large and foreboding to Tobee, but on he goes.

The first thing he notices as he enters the forest is that it gets very dark due to the canopy of leaves from the big trees everywhere.

He knows he must not stray from the flow of the river or he could end up getting lost. The river is moving very slowly, and the deeper he goes into the forest, the more humid it gets as the wind cannot get through the denseness of the trees and their leaves.

Tobee does not see many flowers now; it's just trees and bushes with big green leaves.

The only sound he hears is frogs croaking continuously. Tobee does not like it in here, but he continues on his quest along the river.

He has been travelling through the forest for several hours now, and it is getting hotter by the minute. It is so dark it all seems very eerie. Tobee decides to have a drink of water and find somewhere to rest up before it gets any darker, so he looks around the trees for a small nook to crawl into like he had done before.

He comes across one that is quite high up above the ground, as he does not know what creatures may come out at night here. This forest is making Tobee feel on edge. After he had found this suitable place to sleep, Tobee gets inside. The nook is quite a nice size, not too small or too big, so that no animals or birds can get in.

He does not want to be disturbed in the night. Throughout

the night, he hears the sound of frogs croaking, and this is now joined by the sound of bats squeaking. Tobee is lying there listening to this racket, and it is so hot that it is impossible to sleep. Come morning, he feels absolutely drained; he has only managed to drop off to sleep for about an hour. He decides to take a drink of water and throw some over his face to wake himself up.

Whilst there by the side of the river, Tobee is feeling a bit sorry for himself when, out from behind the trees he sees a deer come down to drink from the opposite side of the river.

Tobee has never seen a deer before. He looks at her lovely big eyes and her beautiful red fur. After a few sips of water, the deer then majestically trots back into the dense forest.

Tobee also notices the gracefulness of her movements; she is like a princess at a royal pageant, to see such beauty brings a tear to Tobee's eyes.

Tobee sits there for a while, just trying to take in what he has just seen.

For the rest of the day, as Tobee travels through the forest, he can only think about the beautiful deer. His thoughts then turned to the darkness in the forest and how every shadow seems to come alive as they flicker with the leaves.

There is a slight breeze that has managed to penetrate the dense forest; to Tobee, this is most welcome as the humidity of the forest was very uncomfortable. Then it starts to rain; it falls down from the leaves above and it comes down at such a rate that he can hardly see anything in front of him, the breeze has picked up as well and is now a ferocious gust, and then as soon as it started, it all stops.

No rain, no wind, the birds have all stopped singing; even the frogs have stopped croaking; just deadly silence. It is like all life is waiting for something, but waiting for what?

Then it comes, a flash of light in the sky, followed a few seconds later by a crackling sound and a loud bang. Tobee

realises straight away, as he has experienced this once before, that it is a lightning strike; however, this seems a lot closer than the last one he saw. Then there's another flash in the sky; there is no gap this time between the flash and the crackling sound, and immediately there is a bang. He sees a tree burst into flames in front of him and all the trees around it also catch fire.

The animals in the forest start to run away from the fire with a look of panic in their eyes, the birds fly off as well. Tobee flies back along the river from where he has just come to get away from the flames. Everything around him is on fire. Tobee is flying as fast as he can. He sees a squirrel jumping from tree to tree, trying to get away. There's a badger below him who is running as fast as he can. A couple of deer gallop by as well.

There is such a commotion; the panic along with the flames, is spreading through the forest. the frogs are all jumping into the river to escape the intense heat, and still, the thunder and lightning continues up above.

A flame shoots out from a bush that has just ignited and hits Tobee on his back leg; the pain is excruciating. He flies down to the river and dips his leg into the water; this soothes his pain, but it is still very painful, but Tobee cannot stop he must carry on to escape the horror of this burning forest.

He flies back along the river as fast as he can until he gets out of the forest and is back at the waterfall, where he sees a hedgehog who is obviously in pain; his paws are all blistered from the heat of the ground. It limps under the waterfall where there is a cavern. Tobee thinks to himself that he will be safe behind there and is pleased that the poor hedgehog will escape anymore suffering.

Tobee must now assail the Hight of the waterfall, so he goes up and up. When he is half way up, he has to fly level for a while as it takes up so much energy to keep flying upwards.

Bees are not as good at flying as birds, who could do it at ease.

After a short time of flying level, Tobee has regained his energy and carries on up the waterfall. He quickly feels his energy sapped from him again, but he can see the top in sight. He thinks to himself, 'just one more effort and he will be there,' Finally, he gets to the top and lands by the side of the rushing river.

When he lands, he topples over to one side as he cannot land properly with his bad leg. He looks over to the other side of the river, where he sees two butterflies who are totally exhausted; they must have flown up the waterfall as well" Tobee thinks to himself.

Tobee then soothes his leg in a nearby puddle and closes his eyes to get some rest.

After a while, he decides to get up. His leg is not hurting so much now, but there is hardly any movement in it. Tobee knows he cannot carry on like this; he will have to return home. He will never be able to land properly again and will only be able to crawl with some difficulty.

His thoughts then turn to his Queen; he feels that he has failed her.

Chapter 10
Sleep Well

Rubee listens to everything that Freebee is telling her. She wipes his brow once more and tells him that she is going to fetch the doctor. Then, she gives him a kiss on the cheek.

When she returns the doctor is with her, holding a bowl of hot liquid. The liquid contains a mixture of boiled plant stems and leaves, The doctor tells him to drink some of it and also to inhale the vapour coming from the rest of it. He also checks Freebees temperature by putting his hand on his forehead. After this, he takes Rubee to one side and tells her, 'We will have to see if the temperature breaks. In the meantime, stay by his side and wipe his brow with a warm damp cloth.' He tells her he will return with another bowl of the solution and that she must make sure that he keeps drinking from it and also inhaling its vapour. Rubee tells him she will stay by his side and administer the liquid to his instructions. Rubee spends the night by his side. They talk a little. Rubee tells him of her life at the hive, and Freebee tells her where he comes from and what he dreams of in life, such as settling down and getting married, Rubee keeps holding his hand throughout the night.

The following morning, the doctor comes in and tells Rubee to go and get some sleep. He will look after him in the meantime. Rubee then gives Freebee another kiss on the cheek and tells him she will be back in a few hours. She goes back to her quarters, feeling emotionally drained. In the short time she has spent by Freebee's side, she has developed feelings for him. She is back on her bed; her thoughts are completely focused on Freebee. Then out of sheer exhaustion, she falls off to sleep.

A little after midday, Rubee awakes. She throws some water over her face and grabs a quick bite to eat. Then, she goes straight to see how Freebee is. When she arrives, the doctor is taking his temperature and giving him more of the medicine that he has prepared. He sees Rubee and says, "Nothing has changed. We will just have to be patient and wait to see how things progress." He then tells her to keep giving him the medicine once an hour and to keep checking his temperature. If anything changes, she is to come and fetch him. Rubee then sits down by his side and takes his hand. She lets him rest a bit then give him some of the medicine to drink and checks his temperature every hour. They talk a little more, and then she lets him rest some more. This continues throughout the day and into the night, with Rubee constantly holding his hand and mopping his brow. Just before daybreak, Freebee opens his eyes, looks up at Rubee with a tear in his eye, smiles at her, and then passes away, Rubee cries out in pain.

The next morning his body is carried out into one of their catacombs and waxed in, this way his body wil be preserved for all the family and friends to come and pay their respects whenever they wish. Rubee spends the whole day crying, but the following day, she takes the journey south, {\avoiding the city, to find Freebee's home to convey the sad news. Freebee had given her accurate details of where he lived; maybe he sensed that things might not end well for him.

Chapter 11
Debbee's Mission

After leaving her hive, Debbee travels over the land as quickly as possible, hardly stopping to eat. She only stopped to get some sleep, and then when she gets up in the morning, she will grab a quick bite of something to eat before continuing on her way. Even when the rain and wind is really fierce, she persists.

After spending the night sheltering under the boulders, Frizzbee looks out and sees that it is raining heavily, so he decides to wait a while until it eases off a bit. He thinks of when he was sitting under the apple tree with Debbee, looking up at the stars and wishing they could fly amongst them.

After spending the whole morning sheltering from the rain, it suddenly stops and the sun emerges. Frizzbee climbs out from under the boulders and flies in circles for a couple of minutes just to stretch his wings and to warm up. He then spots a farmhouse in the distance and wonders if they have any fruit trees or strawberries growing. He fancies something sweet to eat.

The first thing he notices as he flies over to the farmhouse is that there are no fruit trees, but he spots row upon row of grapes growing on vines. Frizzbee has never seen grapes before, he flies down and lands on one of the vines. They have the green grapes on them, so Frizzbee takes a bite, and he instantly loves the taste; they are nice and ripe and so sweet.

After a while, when he had his fill of the lovely grapes, he spots a glass on a table full of drink. Frizzbee thinks to himself," I will have a taste of that, as I need a drink before I leave', so he flies over and lands on the rim of the glass. He

then leans over and takes a sip. At first, he is not sure if he likes the taste of this; it is like nothing he has ever had before. He then has another sip and then another. he is starting to like it. Little does he know that this is homemade wine.

He then decides it's time to leave. He goes to fly off but falls off the rim of the glass and on to the table. He feels weak and dizzy. With a tremendous effort he manages to fly from the table. He is swaying from side to side and then crashes into the side of the farmhouse and falls to the ground behind the heather that is growing there.

Frizzbee has unknowingly got himself drunk!

He then lies down to one side and goes to sleep in a drunken stupor, when he wakes up it is dark, he has wasted the whole day. He has a terrible headache and he feels very thirsty. He decides to never drink from a two-legged creatures' glass again. He then finds a puddle to drink from and gulps down the water, he looks for a more suitable place to sleep for the night and hopes that his head will feel better in the morning. He sees a shed that has a crack in the door, so he decides to sleep there for the night.

In the morning, Frizzbee is feeling a lot more like his old self again, with no headache or dizziness. He takes another sip of water from the puddle he drank from the night before and then flies off in a westerly direction. After a very short time, he comes across a park with so many beautiful flowers. He flies down and tries the flowers that smell so lovely; they are infected with insecticides. Frizzbee sits down and starts to wonder if there is anywhere in this land that has uninfected flowers. If the two-legged creatures have not sprayed their poison on them, then other bees have unknowingly passed it onto them with it being on their legs. While he is sat there, he sees a squirrel running up and down the trees. He has an acorn in his mouth from an oak tree.

The squirrel then gets down on the ground and buries

it. After he has done this, he runs back up the tree and gets another acorn and berries that as well. He keeps doing this over and over again. Frizzbee finds this very strange; he does not know that the squirrel is just putting food away for the winter when acorns and nuts are so hard to find. Frizzbee carries on sitting there, as the sun is quite warm and it is nice to feel it heating up his body. He then spots a blackbird. They may not be the prettiest of birds to look at, but their singing voice is a joy to listen to, so he closes his eyes, feels the warmth of the sun, and listens to the splendid music of the blackbird.

After about an hour, Frizzbee gets up and continues on his journey. He is now going through a small town with houses, roads and some blocks of flats. He decides to travel out of this town as fast as possible. He is now entering open grasslands; his thoughts turn to his Queen, and he feels that he has not been as determined in his quest as he should have been; he has wasted time either sheltering from the rain or being drunk at a vineyard.

He knows that maybe he should not blame himself too much about drinking the wine; he did not know it would affect him like that, but even so, time has been lost. The sun is still shining but a big part of the day was now over. His thoughts then turn to Debbee, Freebee, Hornbee and Tobee. His mind is wandering all over the place. Does Debbee miss him? Is Freebee safe? How far as Hornbee gotten, and what has Tobee been up to? Frizzbee knows he must stay focused on the task in front of him, but without meaning to, his thoughts then turn to home and how he misses being there with Freebee and his friends. His thoughts start to get quite dark, and he starts to wonder how long he will be away or even if he will ever return home. Frizzbee has to stop flying, he sits down in the open grasslands and starts to cry. After a while, he pulls himself together and looks around. The sun is very low in the

sky now, and he is starting to feel cold. He gets up and flies on a little longer, he flies past some horses who are rubbing against each other to keep warm.

He then comes across a large Manor House with stables, and Frizzbee flies into the stables to sleep for the night. A short time later, the horses that he saw in the fields are led into the stables. In a way, Frizzbee is quite happy to have some company for the night as he is feeling lonely.

When Frizzbee wakes up the next day, the horses are gone. He thinks that they must have been led back out into the fields. He looks outside and sees that the sun is high in the sky, he realises that he has slept through the whole morning.

After flying for just under a week, Debbee passes that mine that Frizzbee saw. She does not know it, but she is only about two days behind Frizzbee now. She flies on and comes across the farmhouse, and she also eats some grapes from the vineyard but quickly moves on.

She flies on into the park, where she sees a woodpecker smashing its beak head first into a tree trunk. She has heard of these birds back at the hive, but she thought that they were teasing her. She stares at it for some time in amazement, and she comes to the conclusion that they must be mad and decides to fly on. She comes to a small town, and it is starting to get dark, so she looks for somewhere to sleep. She finds a garden with an evergreen bush running down the side of it and decides to bury herself inside for the night. Her thoughts turn to Frizzbee and then to the woodpecker — what a strange bird.

After flying through a village and more fields, Frizzbee comes across another village with a small church. It is starting to get dark, so he flies up to the bell tower and looks out at the road and the passing car lights. They look like stars shooting across the sky.

There was a cool breeze blowing so he flew back down to find a warm spot inside the church. He saw some curtains that hung down to the floor, so he crawled in between the folds and quickly fell asleep. The following morning, Frizzbee looks out to see a clear blue sky; however there had been a frost overnight and there was a chill in the air. He braced himself to face the coldness of the morning.

Debbee woke up and decided she would have a drink later. She carried on with her journey, and she came towards the fields where Frizzbee first saw the horses. They now have blankets over them to keep warm. She notices that there is a horse trough that was full of water. She took a drink and then went on her way. She went past the stables and then through more fields, on and on she went until she came to a village. She was about twelve hours behind Frizzbee now, there was about an hour's daylight left, so she decides to carry on through the village into an area of more fields and a farm with a chicken pen. She flew in through the roof, and settles down into the upper beams, and watches the chickens settling down on their nests of eggs. Halfway through the night, she was woken with the sound of the chickens making an awful noise. A fox had got into the pen, and the chickens were running all over the place and jumping up and down. This confused the fox; he does not know which chicken to go for. Then there is the sound of the farmer's gun; at the sound of that, the fox fled, but not before grabbing one of the chicken's eggs in his mouth. After this, the farmer fixes the fence around the pen. He then goes back to bed, and the chickens start to settle down and go back to sleep. First thing in the morning just as the sun starts to rise, the cock gives out its morning call and wakes up everyone in the area. Debbee could have done with a couple more hours sleep, but there's no way anyone could sleep through that, so she got up and headed off. It is very cold, and there is a frost on

the ground. After a while, she comes to a village. She saw a church; a strange urge comes over her to look inside. It is still very early in the morning, so she thinks a quick look around wouldn't hurt. There are a couple of big doors at the front of the building, and there is a slight crack in the wood that she can get through.

She flies in and goes straight into a spider's web. she starts to struggle but can't break free. Then she sees a spider coming at great speed towards her. She lets out a scream, and then out of nowhere, appears Frizzbee who flies down and stings the spider, paralyzing it. He tells Debbee to stop struggling, then he cautiously bites his way through the strands of the web that are clinging to her. After he frees her, she throws her arms around him and starts to sob. He tells her, 'It's okay, you are safe now,' she tells him she was so frightened and then gives him a kiss. He smiles and then kisses her back. He then takes her over to a bowl of water on one of the tables and helps her wash off the remaining strands of the web. Once this is done and she has calmed down, she tells him of her plan.

Chapter 12
The Pursuit

Crombee is in his quarters, getting ready to leave the hive and find Hornbee, when Robbee comes in. Robbee has come from another hive whose Queen had died; when they took him in, he was very insecure and relied heavily on Crombee for support.

"I hear you're going," he says, "In a hive it is impossible to keep any secrets; all information just buzzes around in no time." Crombee tells him he will be alright, "but what if the wasps return?" says Robbee. "We gave them a good beating; I don't think they will be back for a while".

Crombee then tries to reassure him that he will be fine and that he has come a long way from that scared bee that first turned up here. He gives him a hug and tells him he will be back as soon as he can, and then flies out of the hive. Crombee looks up to the skies; it is a bit cloudy with a slight breeze blowing in an easterly direction. This is ideal for Crombee, as he is travelling east to catch up with Hornbee, so the breeze should help him on his journey. He passes over fields that are bordered with hedges; one has bales of hay in it (this is where Hornbee took cover one night from the wind and rain). He sees a boy playing with his kite, the breeze sends it fluttering in the sky.

Crombee looks at the boy's face and notices that he seemed so happy. This brings a smile to Crombee's face as to see any young life being happy playing is a joy to watch. There was a dog with him, running around barking with excitement. Crombee can see that the dog really loves the boy. Crombee knows he cannot stay here watching this lovely scene: he must find Hornbee. So on he travels, as the day passes Crombee

notices that the wind has changed direction and is blowing straight at him. This is hindering his progress; he knows it will be getting dark in a few hours, so he thinks that he had better find somewhere to rest up for the night. Right in front of him, he sees the coast. He starts to go along the coastline looking for Hornbee, and then amongst the sound of the wind and the waves he hears Hornbee calling out to him. There he is sitting on a log looking rather perplexed. Crombee flies over to him and asks if he is feeling well. Hornbee tells him that he has to cross the sea or turn back. Crombee tells him of the fight with the wasps and how the Queen has released him from his duties to join him. Then he tells him of a way to get across the sea, Hornbee is all ears to his solution. Two-legged creatures use boats to get across the water. Crombee then tells Hornbee that "we need to wait until it gets dark and look along the coastline for lights; then we will find the two-legged creatures, and then we can look for their boats and stowaway on one".

Hornbee thinks this over; he can find no fault in the plan, and besides, what choice does he have? So, they wait until it gets dark and look for the lights, and then to the right in the distance, they can make out some lights; they seem very dim and flickering as the mist from the sea crosses over them.

So off they go; neither of them has had any sleep, but the cool breeze off the sea keeps them awake.

It was a clear night sky with a full moon, the only sound was the waves coming onto the shore with the mist.

After a few hours, the light seemed to be getting brighter. Crombee turned to Hornbee and tells him, "We are getting closer".

At one o'clock in the morning, they arrive at a harbour with street lights lighting up the whole area. They see some boats, but nothing is moving at this time of the night, so they decide to look for somewhere to sleep until morning.

They see a boat with a waterproof cover over it; they see a small gap that the ropes go through to fasten the cover, so they get in under the cover.

Once inside, they find a warm spot inside the cabin. "That will do for the night," says Hornbee, and they quickly go off to sleep among some cushions.

They woke up with a bump. "What's happening?" cries Hornbee as he rubbed his eyes. Crombee got up and looked out of the cabin.

"We are at sea!"

he exclaimed, then there is a big wave that seems to send Crombee's stomach flying into space and back down to earth again at this horrible feeling, Crombee is then sick on the floor.

Hornbee goes over to him and asks if he is alright. "I think it is sea sickness; I have heard of it before but never had to experience it; I would sooner fight wasps,' says Crombee, as he vomits once more, at this point, Hornbee is also sick; blimey, we are a right pair'."

They both decide to get up top and get some fresh air. They see the waves go up and down; it looks very choppy.

After a while of constantly being sick, the sea starts to calm down, Crombee and Hornbee are feeling very weak, they both decide to take a rest back down in the cabin.

After a couple of hours, they're starting to get their strength; however, they are both feeling very thirsty. They know that they cannot drink the sea water as it is full of salt, but fortunately, up ahead, they spot land, they decide that rather than stay on the boat they will fly ashore.

When they arrive on the island, they look back at the boat to see that it is sailing around the island and is not going to land ashore. Crombee says to Hornbee that it is good to be on solid land. They then look around for some water to drink.

After about half an hour of flying around, they come across a small stream, and take a much-needed drink. Afterwards,

Hornbee says, 'We better wash our legs before we try any of the pollen,' So there they are, washing their legs thoroughly, when Crombee says, 'Right that's good enough, let's go and try some pollen,' They see a field with wild flowers growing. Hornbee goes first, and his eyes light up, 'It's pure!' he says. Crombee then tries some and is smiling with joy after trying it and says, 'You are right!'

Then two bees fly over; one is called Abbee. She has a lovely smile on her face and welcomes them. The other bee is called Albee.

He asks them if they have come far. Hornbee and Crombee both tell them about their quest and how things are where they come from. Albee tells them that the two-legged creatures do not come here as the rocks along the coastline are too jagged for them to bring their boats in, and there are not any long areas of flat land for them to land their planes. Therefore, all the flowers are clean and not infected, Crombee asks, "What do you call this land?" Abbee replies, "Eden."

At this, Crombee falls to his knees and starts to cry, Hornbee also falls to his knees and kisses the ground.

They have found a new home.

Chapter 13
Homeward Bound

When Tobee arrived back at the hive, he requests to see the Queen and was immediately led into court.

The Queen sees him hobble into court, he then bows and says he has failed her. She looks down at his badly burnt leg and immediately orders her personal physician to treat him.

He's taken to the Queen's own private ward, where they put special ointment on his leg and they wrap it in bandages, and then he is told to rest.

A few hours later, the Queen comes in and sits beside his bed. He then tells her about the thunderstorm and the lightning setting the forest on fire, and how the flames shot out and burnt his leg. The Queen holds his hand and tells him that he has not failed her, and that he is a very brave bee.

Frizzbee and Debbee go back to her hive and immediately go to see the doctor. The doctors tell her that the hive council has given permission to proceed with the testing. He then tells her that she should not have flown off without permission. The Queen is very angry. ''You need to report to her immediately, and I will start tests with Frizzbee's blood.''

Debbee goes off to see the Queen, she is led into court. She sees the Queen with the council standing either side of her. Debbee curtsies, "I have been so worried about you." Says the Queen, "if you told me, I would have sent one of my soldier bees with you."

She goes over and gives Debbee a hug, and then asks if Frizzbee was with her. "He's with the doctor who is testing his blood," replies Debbee, "Very well," says the Queen, "now tell me what you have been up to". Debbee tells her about the woodpecker smashing its head against a tree trunk (the

Queen chuckles at this). She then tells her of the grapes she tasted and how lovely they were. Debbee has not really had time to sit back and think about her travels and is getting quite excited telling the Queen about it. She then mentions sleeping in a chicken pen and the fox breaking in, then the farmer firing his gun, and finally getting caught in a spider's web at the church and how Frizzbee saved her life by stinging the spider. "Well, you have had quite some adventure!" says the Queen. "After Frizzbee has had his tests, tell him I would like to see him," and the Queen then lets Debbee go and return to Frizzbee.

The Queen watches Debbee leaves and a smile appears on her face; she recognises young love when she sees it.

Back at the doctor's, things are not going well, it's been two weeks since Debbee was summoned to see the Queen, and the doctor and his staff cannot get Frizzbee's blood to mix with any of theirs; it just does not seem compatible.

Frizzbee goes over to Debbee and tells her "It's not working, I think it's time we went to see your Queen".

They are both led into court, this time the Queen is alone, Frizzbee bows, she summons him forward but tells Debbee to wait outside, she asks Frizzbee how the testing is going, he tells her "It's not working, my blood is not compatible with that of your hives blood".

The Queen remains silent for a while and then says, "You know Debbee loves you very much?" Frizzbee replies that he also loves her with all his heart. "Are you sure?" The Queen says, "I ask you this because I think she is prepared to leave the hive to be with you; she is very young, you know, I need to know you will look after her." Frizzbee replies, "I wish you knew my Queen; she would tell you that I am true to my word, your majesty and I swear I will give my heart and soul to make her happy and to be there for her no matter what

troubles that life may throw at us".

The Queen looks deep into his eyes. After a silence that seemed to last an eternity, the Queen smiles and says that she believes him. She gives him her blessing and then asks him to bring Debbee in.

Debbee comes in looking very worried; both the Queen and Frizzbee smile at her to reassure her. The Queen then tells her that she has given her blessing for Frizzbee to share his life with her.

Debbee starts to well up. "Now then," says the Queen, "what are your plans? Frizzbee takes Debbee by the hand and tells the Queen, "I need to report back to my Queen and tell her about what has happened in regards to the quest the failure of the blood tests, then introduce Debbee and to declare my love for her.".

The Queen then goes over to them, and touches them both on the cheek, and wishes them well. They are escorted from the court.

A few days later, they have left Debbee's hive and have returned to Frizzbee's homeland.

They arrive at the hive and are immediately led in to see the Queen. Frizzbee walks in ahead of Debbee; he then bows, and Debbee curtsies. The Queen listens to what Frizzbee has to say about what happened on his journey, the meeting of Debbee, how Debbee's hive is immune to the infected pollen, and the blood testing.

The Queen looks at Frizzbee and wonders if, instead of looking for uninflected pollen, he went looking for love instead. She does not say anything of this; instead, she beckons Debbee to come forward. Debbee gingerly comes forward, and the Queen asks her if it was true that her hive was immune to the effects of the infected pollen. Debbee is feeling very nervous and does not look up at the Queen; instead, she just looks at the floor and says "Yes, your majesty, it does not affect us." The

Queen replies, "I would like my physicians to test your blood just to see if they can make any progress in the compatibility of your blood with ours. Would this be acceptable to you?" Debbee says that she will do anything to help; "Very well then," says the Queen, "I will see that some quarters are prepared for you, then my physicians will see you in due course."

The Queen turns to Frizzbee and tells him that Tobee has been badly injured, and tells him to accompany her to where he is recuperating. Then she tells members of her staff to escort Debbee to her quarters and see that she has everything she needs.

After a couple of weeks of tests, the physicians confirmed that she has an immunity to the infected pollen; however, they cannot get her blood to mix with theirs, as it is of a different blood type.

The Queen is disappointed at the news, but her opinion of Debbee and her relationship with · Frizzbee has softened as she comes to accept that they really were doing their best to find a solution to their problem. She then summons Frizzbee and Debbee to court and tells them that her physicians could not get their blood to mix. She then quickly changes the subject and asks Debbee about her life, and gets her to tell her in her own words how she and Frizzbee met.

So, Debbee tells her about the Hornet in the apple orchard and how they spent that night looking up at the stars. and how he went off on his mission the following morning, then how she had the idea of mixing their blood. Finally, how Frizzbee saved her from the spider.

The Queen listened intently to Debbee and when she finishes, the Queen smiled and gave them both her blessing. After they had left court, the Queen went back to her private chamber. The effect of the poisoned pollen was making her suffer from fatigue. She hid this from Frizzbee and Debbee, but now that they had gone, she went to bed to rest.

Hornbee and Crombee flew on to the next boat passing the island after they knew the pollen was safe. Once on the boat, they decided to go straight to Crombee's hive first to tell of the good news. However, back at Crombee's hive, the wasps were gathering again.

After the last defeat, Spike, the leader of the Wasps, had gone mad with rage and had ordered another attack, even though they were vastly outnumbered. Sly, his only surviving general, would not dare to defy his leader, and so off they went to charge the hive once more.

The alarm rang out at the hive, with all the bees shouting and getting themselves in position for the oncoming attack. The commander of the bees said, "Right, you know your duty; now give them hell." All the bees dash out, and Robbee struck down three wasps before they had any chance to parry his thrusts. He looked around and sees that they greatly outnumber the wasps; he thinks to himself, "They must be very brave or completely mad!" Then, there in front of him, he sees Spike. The wasp is so full of rage that he is foaming at the mouth; this gives Robbee his answer—they are led by a madman. However, Robbee knows he is going to have to be alert; this wasp did not become their leader without being able to fight.

At first, Robbee keeps out of striking distance, just to get to see his fighting tactics. Spike lunges at him to the left; Robbee dodges this with ease but he can see that he is very fast. Then he pretends to go left again but then changes to the right. Once more, Robbee manages to dodge him. He is glad that he has given himself a bit of distance so that he has time to move out of the Spike's attacks.

These actions of Spike attacking and Robbee dodging goes on for a while, and in this time Robbee is studying his strategies, and he also notices that ha is tiring from his actions and that rage of his is also depleting his energy. Robbee thinks "right it is now or never" Robbee sees Spike come at him

again but instead of waiting for him to strike first, Robbee flies straight at him and then at the last second he moves to the right whilst also going in a slight downward momentum and stings Spike in the right side of his belly, he falls to the ground dead, Sly at seeing this thinks to himself " I am not staying here to get massacred!

And orders what's left of the wasps to flee for their lives.

When Hornbee and Crombee arrive at Crombee's hive, they see all the dead wasps everywhere, they know straight away what has taken place.

Crombee dashes into the hive, quickly followed by Hornbee, to see if everything is alright. Crombee sees his commander, who can see the worry on Crombee's face. The commander smiles and says "Don't worry, the day was ours, and Robbee is a hero; he killed the wasp's leader with some incredible fighting skills and saved the hive. That is the last we will see of them":

Crombee asks where Robbee is now. Well, he has just come back from seeing the Queen, who showered him with praise, and he is now in his quarters taking a well-deserved rest.

Crombee decides to let him rest for now and tells his commander that he wishes for him and Hornbee to have an audience with the Queen, as they have some great news.

The commander looks at him with hope in his eyes but says nothing; he just dashes off to see the Queen. In no time at all, he comes back and says, "The Queen will see you now".

Crombee's Queen was very young, and the effects of the infected pollen had not affected her yet, as it mainly seems to hit the older bees more.

When Crombee and Hornbee enter court, they both bow to the Queen, the Queen then asks for Crombee to introduce Hornbee to her.

The Queen welcomes him and then asks what the great news is. Both Crombee and Hornbee are so excited, explaining

about their journey on the boat and the island of Eden, where they met Albee and Abbee. Then they tell her that the two-legged creatures cannot put their boats ashore because of the jagged rocks offshore, and also why they can't land their planes.

They both pause for a couple of seconds, then Crombee says, "Your majesty, the pollen is uninflected".

The Queen looks at them in disbelief, then a broad smile grows across her face. She then asks if they are welcome there; Crombee replies that they are, but Hornbee needs to let his hive know first, and I will join him, then we will come back here.

Hornbee then explains that we will have to wait for his colleagues who went on this quest to return as well. The Queen is so full of joy and says, "That is fine! in the meantime, we will get ourselves ready to go" The Queen then says, "I hear that the commander has told you about how brave Robbee has been; you may like to go and see him." Crombee replies that he will, the Queen then turns to Hornbee and says, "Thank you. Without you turning up here and speaking to Crombee, none of this would have taken place." Crombee looks at Hornbee and smiles.

Hornbee bows to the Queen and says "it is a pleasure your majesty", Crombee also bows and then they are both escorted from court.

The following morning, after seeing Robbee and congratulating him on his bravery, and also teasing him a bit about being a hero and how he will never be able to live it down, Crombee and Hornbee set off to see Hornbee's Queen.

They arrive back at Hornbee's hive the following day; the weather had been nice and sunny, and their days journey went without any difficulties.

Hornbee wonders if he is the first one back; he's led straight into court, the Queen is sat on her throne and does not stand

to meet Hornbee and Crombee; she is feeling very weak; Hornbee bows and introduces Crombee, who also bows; then he tells her of how they met and how he came with him on his quest; and then they both look at each other and smile.

The Queen sees this and says, "Tell me what you have found," Your majesty," He then blurts it out about the boat journey, the sea sickness and how the two-legged creatures cannot go to the island; he then mentions Albee and Abbe, and then finally the uninflected pollen.

He said all this at great speed; it took the Queen, in her weakened state, a little while to take it all in, and then a smile gradually appears on her face, and then it turns into a broad grin.

She tells members of the court to fetch Frizzbee, Debbee and Tobee, when they arrive, she tells Hornbee to tell them what he had just told her.

On hearing his and Crombee's tale, they go over and shake their hands. Debbee and Crombee are introduced to each other, and then Frizzbee says, "We still have to wait for Freebee."

The Queen says she will send out some of her soldiers to go north in search of him tomorrow, then a member of court enters the room and requests to speak to the Queen.

The Queen beckons him forward, he informs her that there is a female bee called Rubee that has just arrived at the hive. "She requests to see you and claims she has news of Freebee." The Queen senses that something might be wrong and she tells him to lead her into one of the courts smaller chambers, where she will go and see her in a few minutes. She looks towards Frizzbee but says nothing, then she tells them all to remain here and that she will be back shortly.

The Queen walks into the smaller chamber, where she sees Rubee waiting. Rubee curtsies. The Queen gives her a warm smile and then says to Rubee, "I believe you have some news of Freebee?" Rubee immediately bursts into tears. The

Queen goes over to her and puts her arm around her, and tells her to sit down. She then asks if she would like a drink of water. Rubee manages to reply as the tears flow down her face that she would. the Queen gets one of her staff to fetch some water.

After she has had a drink and composed herself a bit, she then starts to tell the Queen what has happened.

Whilst Rubee is telling the Queen about Freebee flying through the city with its smoke and poisonous gases, and how she and her doctor did everything they could to save him, and how she has not stopped crying since, the Queen sat next to her with an arm around her shoulder.

Rubee notices that tears were also flowing down the Queen's face (she feels that she had sent him to his death).

The Queen wiped the tears from her face and then gets a member of staff to fetch Frizzbee. A few moments later, Frizzbee enters the room. He sees that his Queen has been crying; he also sees a female bee that he does not know who has tears flowing down her face. Frizzbee has a sense of fear enter into his body. The Queen tells Frizzbee to sit down, and then tells him what Rubee has told her. The Queen is holding his hand throughout, Frizzbee wails out with grief. At this point, Rubee goes over to Frizzbee and tells him how sorry she is.

Frizzbee manages to thank her for being there for him at the end and for the care she gave him. The Queen then goes out of the room and fetches Debbee; she tells Debbee all that has happened, Debbee dashes into the room to be at Frizzbee's side.

On seeing him, she throws her arms around him; the Queen then beckons Rubee to come with her so that they can be left alone.

She leads Rubee into court, where Crombee, Hornbee and Tobee are wondering what has happened. The Queen

explains all, and of the loving care he received from Rubee.

A silence fell over the court, Tobee was the first to speak. He went over to Rubee and thanked her for what she did and he said to her, "I can see that Freebee meant a lot to you."

Rubee burst into tears again, then the Queen led her to one of her private quarters to rest.

The next day, it is decided that Frizzbee and Debbee will go to Debbee's hive to explain what has happened. They will be going north to attend Freebee's funeral. After that, they will be heading east to live on the island that has uninflected pollen and no two-legged creatures, Crombee and Hornbee will go to Crombee's hive to tell the Queen there that there will be a delay in departing for the island. They will explain that they will be going north for Freebee's funeral. Tobee, due to his injured leg, is to remain with the Queen and Rubee.

Chapter 14
The Funeral

On Frizzbee and Debbee's return, they had brought with them Debbee's Queen and some of her guard's as she insisted on paying her respects. Additionally, when Hornbee and Crombee returned, Crombee's Queen also wished to pay her respects and she brought some of her guards with her. The Queen welcomes them all and gets her staff to find suitable accommodation for everyone.

The following day, Rubee leads them all north to her hive.

The journey is quite long as she leads them round the outskirts of the city. Upon arrival, they are introduced to Rubee's Queen, she is also informed of the island that they will go to for a new life. She speaks to her council, and they agree that a new life on the island would be best.

The next day, after a good night's rest all are led to their catacombs to see Freebee's resting place, then Freebee's Queen reads out a eulogy that she has prepared. She tells them how he was not only brave but he was full of joy and had a big heart that he shared with every bee that he met. At this, Frizzbee starts to tremble as he holds back the tears (Debbee holds his hand). She then recollects her memories of Freebee as a small bee and how he was so inquisitive and always laughing along with his twin brother Frizzbee.

Afterward, she then beckons Frizzbee forward to speak from his heart. She stands to one side along with the three other Queens. Never before had so much royalty been present at the funeral of a commoner.

As Frizzbee stands in front of everyone, he has Debbee at his side to give him support. Firstly, he turns to all the four Queens and thanks them for the honour that they have given to Freebee. He shares the joy that having Freebee in his life. Frizzbee proceeds to recount several stories about their life together, highlighting Freebee's kindness, bravery, and the joy and laughter he brought to their lives and others.

He extends his appreciation to everyone in attendance and specifically thanks Rubee for her tender care of Freebee during his final days. Observing Rubee'!s distress, Tobee joins her for support, and she expresses gratitude for his thoughtfulness. After the funeral, they stay there for a couple of days, where everyone gets to know each other before they set off to the island.

Debbee, Frizzbee and Rubee spend a lot of time visiting Freebee's body in the catacombs.

As the years pass, all three of them regularly return to visit Freebee's resting place to pay their respects.

Chapter 15
The Island of Eden

It had been two months since Freebee's funeral, all the Queens had sent their guards back to fetch the rest of the bees from their hives so that they can all travel together to the island.

On the day that they had arranged to travel to the island, Freebee's Queen goes to visit Freebee alone in his catacomb. She touches the wax covering that encases him and says a few words to him in a very soft voice. She feels his loss deeply, as it was her that sent him on his perilous journey. After a time, she composes herself and joins the others for a trip that will lead to a new life. ·

The journey is led by Rubee at first to lead them back round the outskirts of the city. Once clear, Crombee and Hornbee take the reins for the long journey in a south- easterly direction. Rubee falls back in line behind her Queen as all four Queens lead their own hives out. The first hive to be led out by their Queen behind Crombee and Hornbee is Hornbee's Queen, followed by Crombee's Queen and her hive, then Rubee's Queen and her hive, and finally by Debbee's Queen and her hive.

Hornbee and Crombee knew that they had a big responsibility to lead all these bees to safety: they just hoped that there are no unexpected dangers on the way, then there's the problem of getting so many bees across the water to the island, they might have to do it in small groups at a time, which would mean Hornbee and Crombee having to keep going back and forth to lead them all over.

When they left Rubee's hive, the weather was very cold and wet. However, after a couple of days of travelling southeast, the weather started to improve and the sun broke through, this

was a relief to all the bees; it was nice to feel some warmth on their backs.

From below, they must have looked like a large black cloud passing over as there was nearly 4000 bees on this exodus from their hives to a faraway land.

On the way, they came across some plum trees, so they decided to rest there and eat some of these sweet plums. There were some sheep in a nearby field who were quite startled to see so many bees descending and quickly ran off to the other end of the field.

After they had eaten their fill of the juicy plums, they rested there for an hour and then continued on their way.

Tobee and his Queen needed some assistance along the way from the other bees of their hive due to the Queen's sickness and Tobee's injury.

Once on their way, all the bees felt rejuvenated, and some of them started to hum a tune in their buzzing style. The sun was still shining, and everything was going well. They slept in a field that night, all huddled together to keep warm. When they awoke the next morning, the skies had turned overcast, and the temperature had dropped a few degrees. They took a few sips of water from a nearby stream and then went on their journey once more.

Their mood had changed from the day before as they were all feeling a bit cold, and then there was a really harsh downpour, in no time at all they were all soaked, they then decided to take cover in a nearby wood, Tobee's leg was starting to ache as the damp weather had got into it, and some of the other bees had started sneezing.

It did not stop raining all day, and they were feeling a bit downhearted. They stayed in the woods all day and night, but the following morning, the rain clouds had passed and the sun was out again. So, they set off, and all of them hoped that the rain would not return.

Whilst on the journey, some of the older bees took the time to teach the younger bees about what would be the best pollen to gather on the island, such as honeysuckle and lavender. They said not to be attracted by the big flowers; the plants with plenty of small flowers are best.

The small bees listened with great interest. They were so excited about going to live in a new land and all the adventures they would have. One of the young bees called Hobbee asked if they would see different flowers that they had never seen before. None of the older bees could answer this question as they had never been there before. So, they called over Hornbee and Crombee, who told the young bees that they will mainly see the same flowers that they are used to, but there are also some that will be new to them, and they will be of all different sizes and colours.

The older bees then told the young ones to thank Hornbee and Crombee for their time and advice, all the young bees said "thank you" in unison, Hornbee and Crombee smiled as they saw their excitement was boiling over.

The weather stayed fine for that day along with the next and they were able to make good progress on their journey, and before long they had reached the east coast.

In this time Rubee had helped Tobee to bandage his leg from time to time. She did this out of kindness, as Tobee had been so considerate to her with the grief she was feeling over Freebee's death.

Once on the coast, they waited until nightfall so that they could see the lights that led to the harbour where all the boats were. There was hardly any breeze coming in off the sea, you could hear the waves gently coming In and hitting the coast. It was a very soothing sound, and Debbee told Frizzbee she could quite easily go off to sleep here. Frizzbee smiled and nestled up to her.

A few hours later the sun had started to set and everyone

started to get themselves ready to go to the harbour as soon as the lights were visible, the first one to see the lights was a bee from Crombee's hive called Gumbee, all that sentry duty they did looking out for wasps gave them a very keen eye.

So off they went, following the lights. They reached the harbour in the small hours of the morning. They decided to take some sleep amongst the trees just north of the harbour. and to their amazement there was a cruise ship just off the borders of the coast, Hornbee said "that's it, we can all fly onto the roof and wait for it to sail, it will easily fit us all on top!"

Some of the younger bees looked very nervous as they had never left the land to fly over water. Hornbee and Crombee knew this would be hard for them after their own experiences, but they did their best to reassure them. The following evening, the ship set sail, with all the bees safely on board.

The sea was very calm, and in no time at all, they could see the island of Eden. They waited until the ship started to steer away from the course of the island, and then they set off, still with the Queen at the front of each hive of bees. When they reached the island, they were greeted by Albee and Abbee, who suggested certain parts of the island for them to settle down and live out their lives. There was so much beauty on the island, with all the different types of flowers, that all the bees became very happy there.

A few years later, Tobee and Rubee went up to Tobee's Queen to ask for her blessing to get married. The Queen was pleased for them as they have both suffered so much. After she gave her blessing, they went to Rubee's Queen for her blessing. After they had left, the Queen looks out over the sea and knows one day they will come with their machines, smoke, gases, and all their other poisons. She then wonders how long this world has left, but there is nothing her species can do about that; only one life form can put right the damage that has been done.

THE END